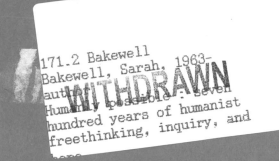

MoooVe OVer!

A Book About Counting by Twos

by KAREN MAGNUSON BEIL

illustrated by PAUL MEISEL

For Patty Figliozzi
K. M. B.

For the Johnsons
P. M.

Text copyright © 2004 by Karen Magnuson Beil
Illustrations copyright © 2004 by Paul Meisel
All Rights Reserved
Printed in the United States of America
www.holidayhouse.com
This artwork was created with acrylic.
The text typeface is Kidprint Bold.
First Edition
1 3 5 7 9 10 8 6 4 2

Library of Congress Cataloging-in-Publication Data
Beil, Karen Magnuson.
Mooove over! / by Karen Magnuson Beil; illustrated by Paul Meisel—1st ed.
p. cm.
Summary: A trolley driver tries to keep track of how many riders he has on board,
but a rude cow on the trolley makes it impossible.
ISBN 0-8234-1736-0 (hardcover)
[1. Cows—Fiction. 2. Behavior—Fiction. 3. Animal sounds—Fiction.
4. Trolley cars—Fiction. 5. Counting.] I. Meisel, Paul, ill. II. Title.
PZ7.B4755Mo 2004
[E]—dc22   2003056798

Here's a plate of thank-yous
for Beth Bini, second-grade teacher,
Altamont Elementary School,
Guilderland, New York, and
Joyce Laiosa, children's librarian,
Voorheesville Public Library,
Voorheesville, New York, for putting
our math fun to the ultimate test: Kids!

There once was a trolley driver who was always on time. At nine he buffed his buttons. At ten he set his watch.

And at eleven sharp he drove his trolley down the road, rain or shine. There was room enough for twenty passengers, so as they boarded, he counted them two by two.

One day he started off as usual. His first passengers were a duet of ducks. He counted them, "Two."

Next he counted a pair of pigs, "Four."

A couple of sheep made "Six," a team of horses, "Eight," and a twosome of geese made "Ten."

6...8...10

At Farm Street and Main was a herd of kids on a class trip.

"Partners!" said their teachers.

"Two at a time!" said the driver, and they all climbed on. "Twelve, fourteen, sixteen, eighteen . . ."

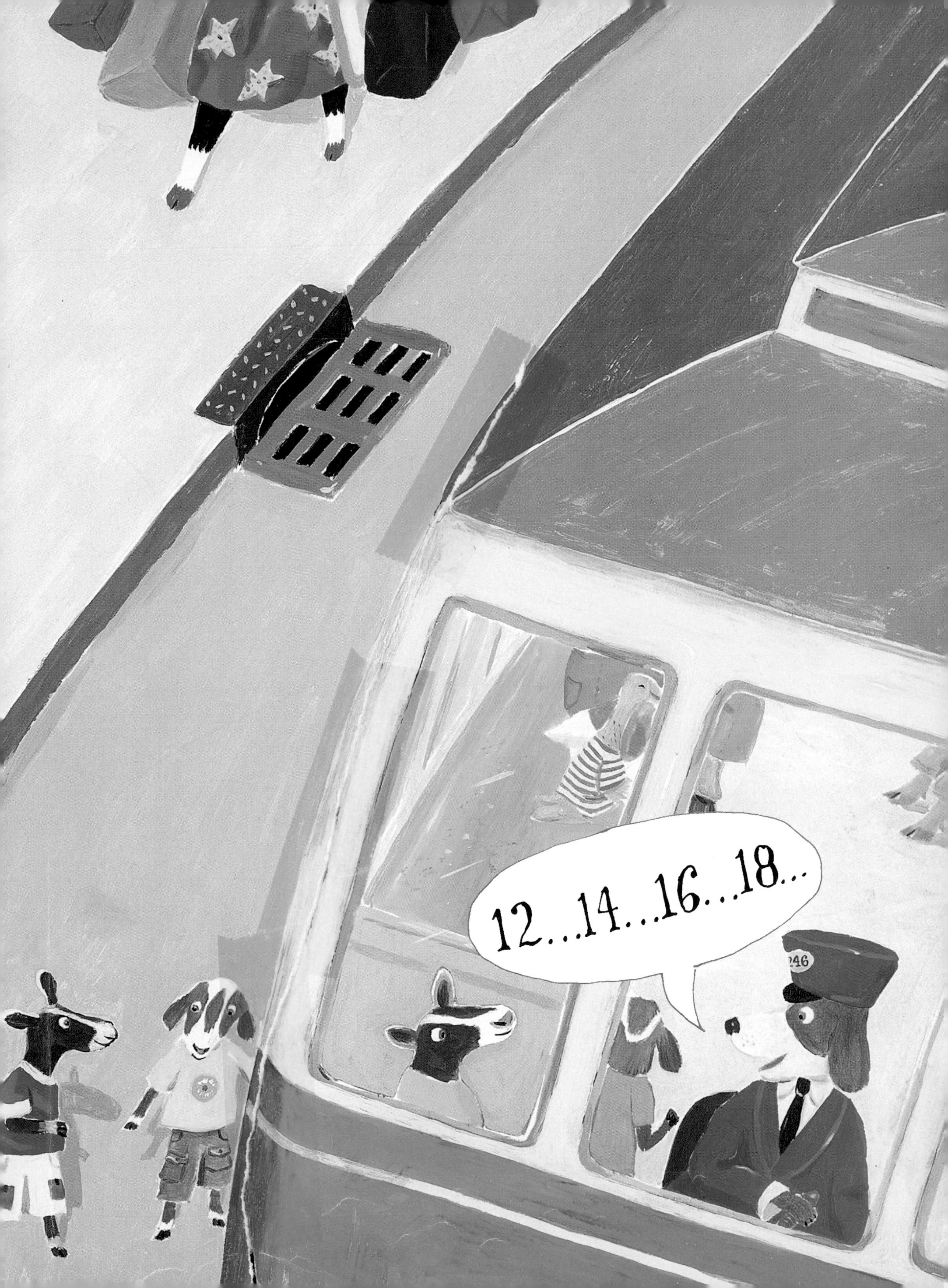
12...14...16...18...

But in the confusion, a cow cut in line. She elbowed her way up the stairs.

She squeezed herself on board. She bumped her bags down the aisle. And for the first time ever, the driver lost count!

". . . Twenty?" he said, shaking his head.
And off went the trolley once more.
"My legs are so tired," said the cow.

"Got enough room?" she asked the sheep.
"Yes, thanks," they said.

"Then mooove over!" said the cow.

"Baaa!"

"Maaa!"

"Then Mooove over!" said the cow.

"There's no room for my bags," said the cow.
"Got enough room?" she asked the pigs.
"Yes, thanks," they said.

"Oiiink!"

"Then mooove over!" said the cow.

"There's no place for my picnic," said the cow.
"Got enough room?" she asked the kids.
"Yes, thanks," they said.

"There's no room for my bags," said the cow.
"Got enough room?" she asked the pigs.
"Yes, thanks," they said.

"oiiink!"

"Then mooove over!" said the cow.

"There's no place for my picnic," said the cow.
"Got enough room?" she asked the kids.
"Yes, thanks," they said.

"Maaa!"

"Then MoooVe over!" said the cow.

It happened again and again.

"MoooVe over!"

"Mooove over!"

"Mooove over!"

"Not very

neeeighborly!"

Now there was only
one passenger, and she
had plenty of room.

The driver glanced back. "Hey! Where IS everybody?"
He stomped on the brake.

As he pulled his passengers back on board, he counted, "Two, four, six, eight, ten, twelve, fourteen, sixteen, eighteen, twenty . . ."

He glared at the cow. "Plus one pushy cow makes

One too many!"

"How rude!" huffed the cow. And she marched off the trolley and straight to the bus stop.

"Yoo-hoo!" she called.
"Got enough room?"

More Fun with *Mooove Over!* Math

Hide & Seek Now you see them, now you don't!

Cover the blue numbers below with fingers from both hands. Start at 2 and read the red numbers. There you go! You've just counted by twos from 2 to 10!

✦ With your fingers over the blue numbers, start at 10 and count back to 2!
✦ Now hide the red numbers. Start with 1 and read the blue numbers.
✦ With your fingers over the red numbers, start with 9 and count back down to 1!

1 2 3 4 5 6 7 8 9 10

Shout & Count Get noisy with numbers!

You can play this with one partner or a whole group. Sit in a circle. The first player whispers "One." The second jumps up, shouts "TWO," then sits back down quickly. The next stays seated and whispers "Three," and on around the circle.

See the patterns? Whisper, shout, whisper, shout. Down, up, down, up. Soft, loud, soft, loud. As the numbers go around the circle, the whisperers get softer until all you hear are loud numbers.

✦ Now go the other way. Start with big numbers and count down to 2.
✦ Count by twos starting with 1.

Draw Your Portrait Mooove over, Picasso!

Draw your picture. If you have a big roll of paper, you can make a life-size picture. Have your friend trace your shape. Now color the clothes and label all the pairs (examples: 2 ears or 2 mittens).

Make Bunny Ears Want a "handy" way to count?

Take a pile of things to count, like pennies, cereal, or paper clips. Put them in groups of twos by giving each counter a partner. Make rabbit ears with your fingers and point out the pairs of counters as you count by twos.

Put on a Play Pretend you're a cast of barnyard critters!

Mooove Over! has parts for 22 actors, plus the narrator. You can add or subtract "kids" or share the narrator's role. Each actor can make a paper plate puppet. Tape on a tongue depressor or stick as a handle. Read and act out the story! *Mooove over! Baaa!*